SUPER SPORTS STORIES FOR KIDS

A Random House book
Published by Random House Australia Pty Ltd
Level 3, 100 Pacific Highway, North Sydney NSW 2060
www.randomhouse.com.au

First published by Random House Australia in 2015

Random House Books is part of the Penguin Random House group of
companies whose addresses can be found at global.penguinrandomhouse.com

National Library of Australia
Cataloguing-in-Publication Entry

Creator: Loughlin, Patrick, author
Title: Super sports stories for kids / Patrick Loughlin; illustrated by James Hart
ISBN: 9780857989666 (pbk)
Target audience: For children
Subjects: Sports stories
          Children's stories
Other Creators/Contributors: Hart, James, illustrator
Dewey Number: A823.4

Cover illustration and design by James Hart
Cover design by Leanne Beattie
Typeset in 14.5/24pt New Baskerville by Midland Typesetters, Australia
Printed in Australia by Griffin Press, an accredited ISO AS/NZS 14001:2004
Environmental Management System printer

Random House Australia uses papers that are natural, renewable and recyclable
products and made from wood grown in sustainable forests. The logging
and manufacturing processes are expected to conform to the environmental
regulations of the country of origin.

Written by
PATRICK LOUGHLIN

Illustrated by
JAMES HART

RANDOM HOUSE AUSTRALIA

FOREWORD

When I was asked to write a collection of short
stories about sport for kids I was excited and a little
worried. How was I going to come up with 12 different
stories about sport? I'd already written pretty much
everything I knew about my favourite sport, rugby
league, in the Billy Slater series. Then I'd written
everything I knew – and a lot that I didn't – about
cricket in the Glenn Maxwell books. Don't get me
wrong, I love writing stories for kids, but I wasn't that
confident about writing about sports I'd never even
watched before, let alone played before.

I'll let you in on a little secret. I'm not very good
at sport. As a child I was even worse. I wanted to be
like the other kids, scoring tries and kicking goals.
I used to daydream about being the sports hero, the
one who wins the game in the dying seconds . . . but

it never really happened (unless you count the many times I beat my dog in backyard footy!).

Then I realised something. By writing these stories I could become the sports star I never was as a kid. That's the great thing about writing stories: you can do anything you want.

I also had a bit of help. Besides countless hours reading about surfing, soccer, netball and BMX racing, I was lucky enough to sit down and chat with Australian karate champion Alice Carrett. I couldn't have written *Pink Belt* without her help and the Italian wouldn't have been right in Marco's Magic Gloves without the linguistic assistance of my colleague and *eccellente* Italian teacher Annette Addabbo.

Some of these stories are about the thrill of competing and winning – or even losing – and some are about the other things that can happen when you're playing sport: the funny things, the weird things, the unexpected things, the amazing things.

Then there are a few stories about things I hope never happen to you when you're out there on the sporting field or track or court or pool or . . . Well, you get the picture.

Some stories are even based on things that really happened to me when I was a kid. My friend did ask me to let him win in a 200-metre race at Little

Athletics and I was attacked by a magpie on that same running track (though not in the same race). Sad to say but my footy team did get beaten 88–0 one game because we only had eight players and, worst of all, I did wet my pants once at school because I was too scared to use the toilets after some older kids told me they were haunted (but please don't repeat that to anyone, it's very embarrassing). Most things, however, are completely made up. I've never had to escape a shark on my surfboard and I'm pretty glad about that.

I hope you enjoy reading these stories as much as I enjoyed writing them. I've tried to make them as fun as possible and I think the same goes with sport. It always gets a bit boring when people take it too seriously. Win, lose or draw, sport is meant to be fun. So if you're a super sports star or just wish you were one like I do, try to have fun out there. It's great to be good at sport but it's better to be a good sport.

The only thing left to say is . . .

On your marks, get set, READ!

Best wishes,
Pat

CONTENTS

WINNING STREAK

Alex Wright stood ready on the diving block. The thick smell of chlorine from the pool below was music to his nostrils.

'On your marks . . .' called the starting official.

Alex bent down low.

'Get set . . .'

Alex looked down the lane and focused on the wall at the end of the pool . . . And that's when he noticed it. Out of the corner of his eye. The little white blur next to his thigh.

In the split second between 'Get set' and the blast of the buzzer, Alex realised what it was. His Speedo drawstring was undone.

MEEEEEEEP!

Alex didn't pause to think. His body took over. He had been trained to launch himself into the pool at the beep of the buzzer, and today was no exception. He dived in . . . And straightaway he felt it.

Oh no, a tiny voice squeaked inside his mind. *Not that. Anything but that.*

But it *was* 'that'. The instant his body hit the water, his Speedos shot from his bottom to his knees. Then, as Alex dolphin-kicked his way to the surface, his Speedos wiggled their way down to his ankles and the little voice inside his head suddenly became a giant one.

I've lost my Speedos! I'm NAKED!

But he hadn't quite lost his Speedos. Not yet. They had slid past both ankles but the knot in the drawstring had caught between the big toe and second toe on his right foot. Any second now, it was going to pull free. Alex had to make a choice: his Speedos or the race.

———

Moments earlier, as he'd stood before the starting blocks, limbering up his arms and legs, Alex had carefully sized up his competition. His main rivals were the three 'I's: Kai, Jai and Gui.

Kai Williams was fast as a bullet through the water and had a good 12 centimetres in height on Alex, which meant that on an even stretch to the wall, Kai would always get there first. Then there was Jai Henley. He was a stocky little ball of power with legs that kicked through the water like jackhammers. You always knew if you were swimming behind Jai because of the whitewash he left in his wake. Finally there was Gui Peters. Gui was a white-haired wonder who was lightning-quick off the blocks. It was as if he had springs in his feet – he always seemed to hit the water before anyone else.

The three 'I's were all great swimmers, yet somehow Alex had managed to beat them two years in a row. Alex's strength wasn't in his start or his height or his power. For Alex, it was all about the race.

According to Coach Hardy, Alex was a natural-born racer. He knew exactly when to sit back and save his energy, and exactly when to kick into overdrive and bring it home to the wall.

'That's why you're a champion,' Coach Hardy had reminded Alex before

he'd walked out for the final of the
50-metre freestyle. 'Sure, those other
kids may be a bit taller or stronger, but
you know how to out-race them, and
that's what you're gonna do today!'

So now, with his Speedos hanging
from his toes and his third State
Championship in the balance, it wasn't
really hard for Alex to decide.

He unclenched his toes and the
Speedos disappeared in his wake.

Alex's ear lifted out of the water as
he turned his head to take a breath.
He heard the roar of the crowd fill the
stadium. Only the roar wasn't screaming
and cheering like in most of his races,
it was a flood of laughter. The crowd was
in hysterics.

They're laughing at me. They can see my . . . my bottom, whimpered the tiny voice inside Alex's head. *Why did I wear Speedos in the first place? I should have worn Skins, like the others.*

Most of the other swimmers wore skin-tight knee-length Skins. But not Alex. Coach Hardy had told him that by racing in Speedos at the State Championships, he would be a full second or two quicker wearing Skins at the Nationals, giving him the edge over the other State swimmers who would see Alex's personal best and underestimate him.

Another voice leapt into Alex's head and elbowed the little one out of the way. It was Coach Hardy and he wasn't happy.

'Alex, you big nong, it's just a bottom! Everyone's got one. Now stop whimpering and race. You're falling *behind*, boy (no pun intended)!'

To his horror, Alex realised that Coach Hardy's voice was right. As he turned to take his second breath, he glanced across the lane and saw that he was at the very back of the pack of swimmers. Alex was in last place with 30 metres to go.

Last place? said the little voice in his head. *Don't tell me you just lost your Speedos for nothing. Coach Hardy's right. You* are *a nong!*

A bolt of electricity shot from Alex's brain into his limbs, shocking them into action. Not winning due to a Speedo mishap was one thing, but coming last was another thing altogether. It just was not an option, bare bottom or not.

Focus, Alex, you've got a race to win, he told himself.

He took another breath and his ear broke free of the water once again. He could hear the crowd screeching and screaming with laughter. He could see them now, too, in his mind – laughing till they were red in the face, slapping their thighs, elbowing each other and falling off their seats. He would be the laughing stock of the junior swimming circuit, the butt of every joke (no pun intended . . . well, maybe a little bit intended).

But Alex blocked out the roaring laughter of the crowd that filled his ears each time he lifted his head out of the water.

And he blocked out the sensation of cold pool water swirling around his Speedo-less privates.

Instead he stared down at the black line below him, drawn along the bottom of the pool. He focused on winning the race – his third State Championship win in a row. His arms churned through the water like windmills. His feet kicked with the blurring speed of a hummingbird's wings.

He quickly moved past three swimmers. With 20 metres to go, he was into fifth place and a body length behind the leaders. With ten to go, he had pulled even with Kai and Jai and was gaining on Gui. With five metres to go, Alex went supernova.

When his fingers touched the wall, no one was with him. He had left them all for dead. He'd won his third State Championship.

Then, as he leapt out of the water, his right fist pumping the air in celebration, he remembered something.

He was naked.

Quick as a flash, Alex tore his swimming cap from his head and covered himself.

But it was too late.

The crowd had seen *everything*.

As the other swimmers touched the wall, Alex sank back down into the water and sheepishly looked around the pool's stadium. To his great surprise, the crowd wasn't howling in laughter or slapping each other's back in hysterics or rolling around on the floor in stitches. They were jumping up and down and cheering!

Alex breathed a sigh of relief. Maybe he wouldn't be the butt of every joke around every junior swimming pool after all . . .

'Alex, you little legend, what a race!' shouted the real Coach Hardy from the side of the pool. 'That was a full point-five of a second off your personal best. From now on, son, you're swimming *every* race naked!'

BOXING DAY BLUES

I hate Christmas.

I know it sounds a bit weird for a kid to say that they hate Christmas, but I do. Actually, what I really hate is the day after Christmas. Boxing Day.

Still weird though, right? Why would a kid hate Boxing Day? Well, Boxing Day may be great for you – you get to play with your Christmas presents, eat leftovers and watch the first day of the Boxing Day Test match on telly. But for me Boxing Day means one thing: the Reynolds Family Christmas Picnic.

You see, every Boxing Day my family heads to Katta National Park for a Christmas get-together with my dad's entire family. It doesn't matter if it's 45 degrees or pouring rain, we never miss a Boxing Day picnic.

My family's become a bit fanatical about the picnic. Every year we leave home at eight o'clock in the morning so we can get the best spot, before anyone else claims it. The other thing my family is fanatical about is the Boxing Day Reynolds Family Cricket Match. And that's the real reason I hate Boxing Day. That and my Uncle Pat.

Everyone in my family loves Uncle Pat. They think he's hilarious. Not me. I don't find Uncle Pat funny at all. Every time I see Uncle Pat he says the same thing. And everything he says has an action that goes with it.

'Hello Joe,' he says, crushing my hand in a manshake till it goes numb.

'What do you know?' he says as he squeezes my nose.

'Haven't seen you round *'ere* for a while,' he adds as he yanks my ear.

'Come on, Joe, give us a smile!' he says while he grabs my mouth and pushes my lips up at the sides.

'What's the matter, cat got your tongue?' he asks. He pushes my cheeks out till my tongue pops out of my mouth.

'Or were you just born with a stick up your bum?' And that's when Uncle Pat gives me a wedgie.

Every time he does it everyone in my family laughs.

But that's not the worst thing about my Uncle Pat. The worst thing is when he plays cricket.

Uncle Pat is really good at cricket.

He used to play for the Green Hill District First Grade team. So whenever Uncle Pat is batting, no one can ever get him out.

I'm serious. All my uncles and cousins and I try our guts out but he just slogs us around the park. It's so annoying. He doesn't even use two hands. He usually stands there with a beer in one hand and swats the ball for a six like he's not even trying. Then, after a while, he'll say, 'Get ready, Joe, here comes a catch!' and he'll put one up in the air. But it always goes just over my head, or too far to the left or the right or just short. No matter how fast I run, I always end up diving in the dirt and missing the ball.

Or worse, I get a hand to it and drop it anyway. Then Uncle Pat will say, 'Bad luck, Joe. Maybe you'll get the next one.' But I never do. And usually after an hour or so of getting belted all around the park and dropping catches, me and my cousins get bored and the game gets abandoned.

But that's still not the worst of it. The worst thing is what happened last Boxing Day.

Last year for Christmas I asked for my very own cricket bat and Santa brought me one – a Thunderbolt 360. It was beautiful and all I wanted to do was to get out there and play. So on Boxing Day I asked Dad if I could bring my bat to the park. He said it would be okay.

I was so excited. Till I saw who was
bowling. It was Uncle Pat. And he
was almost as good with the ball as
he was with the bat.

The first ball whizzed past me. I never
even saw it. It struck the old metal bin we
used as our makeshift wicket with a loud
clang.

'Stick around, Joe,' said Uncle Pat.
'Can't get out first ball, you know.'

So I stayed in bat. But only for
another 20 seconds, because the second
ball was even faster than the first.

CLANG!

'Guess it's my turn,' said Uncle Pat.
He took my brand-new bat off me and
spent the next half-hour smashing the

ball over our heads, as usual. Then he said something that I'll never forget.

'Hey Keith, grab your leather ball,' Uncle Pat said to my cousin. 'We'll put a few cherries on this thing.'

Before my dad or I could say anything, my Uncle Craig, who was bowling, had swapped the tennis ball for Keith's six-stitcher and fired it down the pitch at Uncle Pat.

CRRRAAACK!

It was the worst sound I've ever heard. Uncle Pat held up my Thunderbolt. There was a giant split down the middle.

'Um . . . yeah, you really have to oil these bats before you use them,' he said.

He promised to replace it but it never happened. Every time I saw him, he always said he'd get around to it and eventually I just gave up asking.

So that's why I hate Boxing Day.

But today is different. Today is the Boxing Day that I get my revenge. I've been planning it for months.

You see, I have this friend at school, Jake Townsend, whose dad works in research and development for an industrial adhesive company. One day when I was over at his place, he showed me a new product his dad was working on: Spray-On Magnet. It works exactly like spray-on glue but once it dries it makes any surface magnetic.

That's when I got my idea. It was simple, but it was pure genius.

I couldn't wait to try it out.

One afternoon Jake and I took an ordinary tennis ball and sprayed it with the Spray-On Magnet. We didn't just spray it once, though. We sprayed it once, waited for it to dry, then sprayed it again. And again. And once more for luck. Then we threw it at Jake's metal fence. It stuck! In fact, it's still there. We couldn't budge it.

We grabbed another tennis ball and came up with a new plan. Would it work if we only sprayed it once? It did. Perfectly.

I hid the ball in the top of my wardrobe and waited for Christmas – or, more precisely, for Boxing Day.

Finally it's here. Today's the day that Uncle Pat will get a cricket match he'll never forget.

————

We get to Katta National Park bright and early in the morning. Uncle Pat, Aunt Mel and their kids are already there. Uncle Pat is wearing a bright pair of designer board shorts, worn-out thongs and a singlet that has 'LITTLE RIPPER' printed on it.

He greets me with the usual routine. I play along and don't even wince when he ends with the wedgie. I'm focused on one thing and one thing only.

After lunch my dad says, 'Who's up for cricket?'

My cousins and uncles and my dad all head out to field.

'Come on, Joe, don't be slow,' calls Uncle Pat.

'Coming,' I say, as I grab my secret weapon and push it into the pocket of my cargo shorts.

But when I get out on the field I stop dead. Something is very wrong.

'Where's the metal bin?' I ask.

'Don't need it anymore, Joe. Aunt Mel got me this new beaut esky for Christmas,' says Uncle Pat excitedly. 'It's got a built-in wicket that pops out of the lid. Brilliant, hey?'

I stare in disgust at Uncle Pat's brand-new, all-plastic esky with the

built-in stumps. I take the magnetic
tennis ball from my shorts and toss
it away.

Just like that, my plan is ruined.

Uncle Pat soon gets his turn at
batting and no one can get him out.
He's smashing fours and sixes like
there's no tomorrow.

I can't bear it. It's worse than every
other year combined. Each time I chase
down another boundary from Uncle
Pat's bat I feel as if my own heart has
been tossed down the pitch and whacked
for six.

Then I notice something. When
Uncle Pat opens up the esky to grab
himself another can of beer, my

26

abandoned magnetic tennis ball begins to roll towards the esky.

What? Magnets aren't attracted to beer cans – they're made of aluminium . . . Then I look closer. This year Uncle Pat has treated himself to an esky-full of fancy, vintage-looking beers. Beers in steel cans. *Eureka! My plan could still work!*

I inch my way over to my tennis ball, pretending to swap fielding positions so that I don't raise any suspicions. When I get to it, I fake tying up my shoelace but instead shove the ball back into my pocket.

I wait until my dad finishes his over then casually ask, 'Can I have a bowl, Dad?'

'You can't do worse than me,' he says, and he tosses me the tennis ball.

I walk away from the bowler's crease, which is marked by an ice-cream tub lid, and pretend to measure my run-up. Just before I turn around to bowl, I swap the tennis ball in my hands for the one in my shorts.

I turn around but then I notice something else. Uncle Pat has a beer in his hand.

'Give us your best, Joey,' Uncle Pat calls.

'Maybe you should put that beer down first. I'm feeling lucky today, Uncle Pat,' I shout back.

'Oooh! Slow Joe's gonna give me some heat!' He puts the beer on top of the esky, just behind where the stumps stick up.

Perfect.

I run in fast, but not too fast. I have to bowl this right on line to work.

Uncle Pat is bumping his bat on the pitch and smiling.

I release the ball and watch it fly down the pitch.

Come on! Work, ball, work!

The ball bounces right in front of Uncle Pat's thongs. He pulls the bat back, ready to send the ball rocketing to the sun. But when he swings, the ball is gone.

Clang!

It strikes the top of the stumps, sending Uncle Pat's beer flying. It sticks to the esky for just a second, attracted to the cans inside, then slides to the ground.

'Howzat!' screams my dad. 'You've done it, Joe! Clean-bowled!'

I go and retrieve the ball, hoping no one notices me slipping it back into my pocket.

My cousins and uncles rush in and high five me. No one can believe it.

My Uncle Pat can't believe it either. 'How did you . . . How did you do that?'

'Well, Uncle Pat,' I say with a smile, as I hand him back what's left of his beer, 'you've gotten fat!' I poke him in his beer belly.

'Maybe you need to cut down on the beer.' I tap his beer can with my magnet-coated tennis ball and the can flies out of his hand, spilling beer all down his 'LITTLE RIPPER' singlet.

'Although it's good to see you're still *'ere*!' I give his ear a big tug. It feels great.

'Wish I had time to stand round and chat but, if you don't mind, it's my turn to bat.' I take the bat out of his hand and Uncle Pat just stares at me, his mouth hanging open like one of those clowns at Luna Park.

'There's no reason to be so glum,' I say, using my other hand to push his lips up to make a smile.

'Unless you were born with a stick up your bum!' And with that I reach around to Uncle Pat's designer board shorts and give him the mother of all wedgies.

I take my place at the crease and get ready to bat. For the first Boxing Day ever, I'm actually happy. And you want to know something? I'm even looking forward to next year. I can't wait.

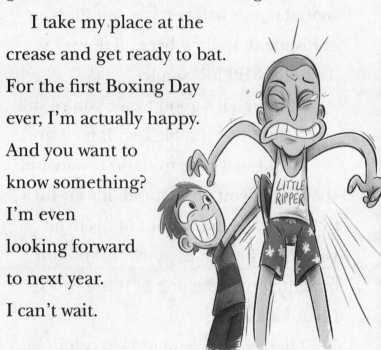

PINK BELT

'Boooooooo! Rubbish! Get her off!'
called a voice from the back of the school
hall as Alice Pepper stood on the stage in
her white Gi and black belt, a shiny new
gold medal around her neck. She had just
delivered a three-minute presentation at
the school assembly about her National
Karate Championship win and clearly not
everyone was impressed.

'Right, who was that?' demanded Deputy Principal Mr Scollard. 'That's completely uncalled for. We listen with respect!'

But Alice didn't need to ask who it was. She would recognise that high-pitched weaselly voice anywhere. It belonged to Zachary Peters, the biggest, nastiest, most weaselly boy at Green Hill Primary School. He did karate, like Alice, except Zach went to Kublai Khan Dojo while Alice was a student at Poppa Chan's Karate Academy.

Sports karate is not what everyone thinks it is. First, there's no 'Hiya!' or karate chops. As Alice's sensei Dan would say, 'Chops are for cooking on barbecues!'

Second, karate is not that dangerous.
You fight for points, not to inflict pain.
In junior karate, you weren't supposed
to punch or kick with full force. This was
called pulling your punches. Instead,
points were given when you demonstrated
technique, timing and sporting attitude.
One point for a tsuki (a punch) or uchi
(a strike), two points for a chudan-geri
(a kick to the body) and three points
for a jodan-geri (a kick to the head) or
a throw.

Zach, however, seemed to find it hard
to control his aggression. He'd made it
to the State Championship but didn't
get through to Nationals because he
kept getting penalised for not pulling his

punches. Alice hadn't been surprised.
Even at school he was nasty. When
Alice had achieved her black belt in
Year Three and brought it in for show
and tell, Zach had waited till Alice was
walking back to her seat then mumbled
just loud enough for Alice to hear: 'Girls
should wear pink belts.'

Alice never forgot it.

Now he was at it again. But Alice
wasn't going to just let it go this time.
She was going to settle this once and
for all.

At recess she and her friend Jenny
marched right over to where Zach and
his friends were hanging out by the
bubblers.

'Zachary Peters!' she called. 'I know it was you who booed!'

'So? What are you gonna do about it, Pepper?' spat Zach.

'Saturday at Poppa Chan's. You and me in a proper match,' said Alice. 'Loser has to wear a pink belt for life.'

Zach's eyes widened and his friends stood there, waiting to see what Zach would say. In the end there was only one thing he could say.

'You're on! But not at your wimpy dojo. We fight at Kublai Khan.'

'Fine,' said Alice. She couldn't back out now.

'Better get yourself a pink belt,' spat Zach. 'You're gonna need it!'

———

When Alice stepped into Kublai Khan Dojo on the day of the fight, she had to stop for a second.

'You okay?' asked Jenny.

'I'm fine.' She wasn't, of course. Her legs were all wobbly and her head was giddy. She felt as if she was about to throw up.

'You look like you're about to throw up,' said Jenny.

'Thanks a lot.'

'I don't know what you're worried about. You're totally going to win.'

Alice smiled at Jenny's vote of confidence.

'Unless . . . you know . . . you don't,' added Jenny.

'Maybe you should just stop talking now,' said Alice. Jenny shrugged, and as they walked up the stairs to the sparring area, Alice nearly did vomit. It looked as if nearly all of Year Five was there waiting.

'Jenny, who did you tell about the fight?' asked Alice.

'No one!' protested Jenny. 'Just Leah. And Shanice. And maybe a few others . . .'

'Great,' said Alice as she pulled on her red gloves, still in shock that her grudge match with Zach had somehow become the Year Five social event of the year. But her disbelief was interrupted by a weaselly voice.

'Can't believe you actually showed, Pepper! You must have a death wish!'

'Yeah, well I'm here,' said Alice. It wasn't much of a comeback.

As she took her stance behind the line inside the fighting area, she began to think that maybe Zach was right. He towered over her. How had she ever thought she could beat him?

40

Then she remembered the words
her sensei Dan had spoken before her
National Championship match. 'It's
not about how big you are, it's about
how smart you are. A karate match is
like a game of chess. You have to have a
strategy.'

So what's my strategy? wondered Alice
as she performed the shomani-rei, the

bow to the corner of the room to show
respect to the school, before she and
Zach bowed to each other.

'You're dead,' mouthed Zach.

Strategy one: don't die.

They bowed to Zach's sensei, who
would ref the match.

Strategy two: don't let him force you out.
Strategy three: be brave. Strike first.

'Hajime!' the ref called.

The fight began.

There were three minutes on the
clock. Three minutes to decide who
would win and who would be wearing
a pink belt for life.

Zach didn't waste time. He went after
Alice straightaway with a flurry of punches

that she was able to dodge by twisting her body and springing backwards. But suddenly she was on the edge of the blue mat and close to the red penalty area.

'*Kiiiiiai!*' cried Alice, and she went on the attack, throwing her own combination of punches.

But Zach was able to block her. Before she knew it, he had turned sideways and clocked her with a jab to the head. Alice staggered backwards. Zach hadn't pulled his punch at all.

The ref didn't penalise Zach, though. Instead he awarded him a point.

Zach's friends all cheered but some of the crowd who knew more about karate booed.

Alice shook it off and took up her place behind the line.

'Come on, Alice!' called Jenny.

Alice nodded. She had to be more careful.

'Hajime!' the ref called again.

Alice sprang to her toes, bouncing back in anticipation of another Zach attack. Zach didn't disappoint. He pushed forward, testing her defence with some feigned punches before going all-out with a roundhouse kick aimed straight at Alice's face. Alice saw it coming and swept his leg away with a right block that unsteadied Zach and sent him stumbling sideways.

'*KIIIIIIAI!*' She counter-attacked with

a side snap kick straight to Zach's solar plexus.

It was an obvious two points but the ref didn't score it.

No way! thought Alice. But there wasn't time to complain. Zach recovered quickly and tried a low roundhouse kick. This time Alice couldn't twist her body out of the way. Zach's foot hit her square in the chest and sent her sprawling across the mat.

'OOOOOHHHHH!' gasped the crowd.

The ref scored Zach two points. He was up 3–0 with less than a minute left on the clock.

If I'm going to score I have to do something big, thought Alice, as she took up her stance behind the line.

Zach didn't attack this time. He might have been a weasel but he wasn't stupid. He had the lead. He could hang back and wait for Alice to come to him. Alice didn't have much choice; she needed points.

Be brave, she told herself. *Brave but smart.*

She made her move with a stutter step backwards that drew Zach in. He saw his chance, reaching low to grab her Gi for a three-point take down. It was just what Alice wanted. She stretched her right leg up and over and executed a perfect scorpion kick to Zach's head.

'Yes!' yelled Jenny from the crowd. 'You have to score that, ref!'

Jenny was right. The ref awarded her three points. It was locked up at three all with 32 seconds on the clock. The next point would win it.

Alice got behind her line and faced off against Zach for the final time. He looked mad. His face was twisted into a desperate snarl. He didn't look like a weasel anymore. He looked like a snarling werewolf.

He's going to attack. But will it be with the fist or the foot? wondered Alice.

'Hajime!' called the ref.

Alice got ready.

'*Kiiiiiai!*' screamed Zach. He launched himself at Alice with a double punch followed by a stinging roundhouse kick. Alice blocked the double punch with an outward sweep of both hands then snapped her head backwards as Zach's foot knifed at her face.

What happened next stunned Alice, Zach and the whole crowd.

Alice shot her hands forward and grabbed Zach's foot midair.

Zach's mouth fell open in shock as Alice twisted his right leg down with her forearm and sent him crashing to the floor.

'*Kiai!*' cried Alice, as she followed through with a punch to the head. But, unlike Zach, Alice did pull her punch. Just enough to tap him lightly on the nose. Then she tweaked it. 'Gotcha,' she said.

Zach thumped his fist on the floor.

'Woohoo!' screamed Jenny.

The ref scored Alice three points then blew his whistle to call time. Alice had won.

Reluctantly, Zach got up. 'All right, just give me the belt and get it over with,' he mumbled.

Alice pulled from her bag a fluffy pink belt she'd taken from her mum's old bathrobe. She held it out for Zach. He shuddered.

But once again Dan's voice popped into her head. 'Always respect your opponent.' It was the number-one rule in karate.

Alice looked at Zach's miserable face, then tied the pink belt around her own waist.

'You know, I think it suits me better,' she said. 'I might keep it.'

Zach realised that Alice was letting him off the hook and gave a smile. Not a weaselly smile. Just a normal-kid smile.

'Thanks, Alice,' he said, just loud enough for her to hear. 'You're all right.'

And for Alice, hearing Zach say those words was like winning her gold medal all over again.

TAKING A DIVE

'Let me beat you,' Bradley whispered
across the track.

Robbie Willis couldn't believe his
ears.

Both boys were standing in their lanes waiting for the starting pistol to fire for the 200-metre final. It was the moment Robbie had been waiting for all summer. The 200 metres was his best event and today was the Green Hill district Little Athletics Gala Day – the biggest day of the season.

'No way,' said Robbie finally. 'Why should I?'

'My dad's here. He used to be a state champion. If I come last he's gonna kill me. Just this once, take a dive,' pleaded Bradley.

'Take a dive'? Who even says that? wondered Robbie. It was the sort of thing mob guys said to boxers in crime shows.

Robbie pushed his blond fringe back out of his eyes and looked over at the crowd standing by the finish line. He could see Bradley's dad waiting there expectantly.

'Come on, Robbie. *Please!*' whispered Bradley as the boys took their marks.

But the starting pistol fired before Robbie had time to give it another thought. Suddenly they were off and running.

It was a bad start. Robbie had been so distracted by Bradley that he had been slow off the mark. What was worse was that Bradley was about four strides in front of him. Even worse than that was that all the other boys were *way* far out in front of them both.

Robbie pushed Bradley out of his mind. What he'd asked wasn't fair. Why should he take a dive? This was Robbie's race, too. He focused on getting into his stride and keeping himself from running flat out. The trick with the 200-metres race was that you needed to time your run so that you hit your top speed between the 100- and 150-metre mark.

As he hit the turn, he pulled back some of the lead from the outside runners, although they still looked miles ahead. He broke even with Bradley and saw him turn his head. That desperation was still there in Bradley's eyes.

Robbie felt a pang of sympathy. Maybe he didn't need to win today . . .

But before Robbie could make up his mind, he saw something that changed the game. On the track ahead of him was a familiar shadow. And it was growing bigger and bigger.

Maggie was back.

Maggie was the local magpie and she had terrorised the Little Athletics squad for the past three seasons. Her nest was in one of the gum trees that lined the fence of the track. She took great delight in dive-bombing the runners when they got too close to her tree.

This year Maggie hadn't been spotted, much to the relief of the athletics squad. But just that morning, perfectly timed to ruin Gala Day, Maggie had returned, attacking a poor little Under Eights girl, who had blonde pigtails, as she walked across the carpark.

It seemed that Maggie hated blonde hair. And she hated Robbie's blond hair most of all. He had been attacked no less than six times in his three years as a Little Athlete and each time was just as terrifying as the last. Just last year she had pecked him right behind the ear, leaving a jagged arrow-shaped scar.

Now Maggie had returned to terrorise her favourite blond victim.

'Magpie!' screamed Robbie.

As the words left his lips, he heard that terrible noise. *Whoop, whoop, whoop.* It sounded like the whirling of helicopter blades or a low-flying razor-sharp frisbee whizzing right past his ears.

Both he and Bradley let out a spontaneous yelp and slipped their legs into top gear. Nothing motivates like fear, and nothing is scarier than the beating wings of a magpie on a mission. Robbie pushed his legs as hard as he could. Bradley was right there beside him. They weren't just running to win anymore. They were running for their lives.

Suddenly they were overtaking the other runners!

But Maggie wasn't interested in the others. She had a certain long-legged blond boy in her sights.

The first swoop was at the 125-metre mark. Robbie felt Maggie's wings whoosh past him as her beak thumped the back of his head. It felt as if he'd been hit by a rock.

Robbie almost burst out of his skin. Suddenly his legs found another gear and he was hurtling down the straight of the track like a human rocket – a very scared human rocket being chased by a black-and-white missile.

He was overtaking everyone now. At 150 metres he moved into third place, with Bradley just a step behind. Normally at this point his chest would start to burn but today he didn't feel anything. He was too busy worrying that Maggie was circling back for a second pass at his tempting blond head.

Sure enough, with 25 metres to the finish line, he heard it again.

Whoop, whoop, whoop.

Bradley must have heard, too, because he let out a wind-muffled whimper and caught up with Robbie.

'Run, boys, run!' yelled a lady from the crowd.

With ten metres to go they were dead

even for first, just as Maggie made her final dive at Robbie's head.

There were cries from the spectators as they saw the bird spearing down on the two boys, her beak like a bayonet. Robbie and Bradley dived towards the finish line and Maggie missed Robbie's ear by a centimetre.

The bird pulled up at the sight of the track officials waving her away and burst back up into the sky.

In a photo finish it was Maggie first by a beak, followed by Robbie in second by the tip of his blond head, and Bradley in third.

Not that anyone was really focused on the result. They were all too concerned for the two boys who had crashed to the ground after Maggie's last dive.

'You okay?' asked one of the track officials.

'I think so. You okay, Robbie?' asked Bradley.

Robbie felt the back of his head where the magpie had struck him. There was a spot of blood but nothing too serious. 'Yeah,' he replied. 'Stupid bird.'

'But it did make me run faster,' said Bradley, laughing.

'Me too,' said Robbie.

'Thanks for not letting me win,' said Bradley. 'I should never have asked you to do that. Sorry.'

'That's all right. But I think you should thank Maggie, not me,' said Robbie.

'Fantastic race, boys!' said Bradley's dad as they left the track.

'Thanks, Dad,' said Bradley.

'Although I'm a little disappointed in both of you,' added Mr Lewis.

'What? Why?' asked Robbie.

'You got beaten by a bird,' said Mr Lewis, with a grin.

Robbie and Bradley rolled their eyes. There was just no pleasing some people.

KILLER WAVE

Here I am, walking on water, as if there's nothing else in the world except me.

And my surfboard.

And the wave.

And the shark.

Oh yeah, I forgot to mention. There's a shark chasing me. A great white, to be precise. And when I say 'great', I don't mean 'good'. I mean 'HUGE'. He's probably a 20-footer, and I suspect he wants to make me his breakfast.

But let me take a sec to go back and explain exactly how I got into this mess. My name is Sam Burke and before I decided to get eaten by a shark I was about to become the Under 12s Junior Girls State Champ – in other words, the best girl grom in the state. A grom's a grommet, by the way, in case you're a non-surfer type, and a grommet's a kid who can shred waves like a whipper snipper shreds grass. I don't want to sound like a big head or anything but trust me, I can. I've been surfing since I was four.

Today was going to be my day. The

day I caught the perfect wave and took out the title. I could feel it as soon as I got to the beach and saw the lush sets rolling in. The conditions were perfect. I couldn't wait to get out there and rip it up.

I pulled on my wettie and added a little more wax to my brand-new custom surfboard. (My older brother Corey made it for me. He designs boards for a living and he did an awesome job on mine. It has killer rails and this sweet lightning bolt right down the middle.)

That's when I made my big mistake.

I pulled on my headphones for a little chill-out music and closed my eyes. When I heard the horn sound for my heat, I zipped up my wettie and ran into the surf. I was totally amped. Just before I duck dived under the whitewash, I could hear everyone on shore cheering me on, screaming my name.

'Sam! Sam! Sam!'

It wasn't until I paddled out past the first set of breakers that I realised something wasn't right. The horn went a second time. And it sounded a little different to how it usually sounded. It was more like a warning siren.

I looked back over my shoulder to the shore and saw a whole bunch of people waving and screaming. They weren't screams of encouragement. They were high-pitched squeals of fear.

But why would they be afraid of me
heading out to catch a wave?

Oh.

Right.

I looked in front of me and saw
the fin.

It was enormous. And it was heading
right my way.

Instinctively I pulled my feet out of
the water and curled up my legs. Then
I looked up again for the fin.

It was gone.

I looked all around me.

Nothing.

That could mean only one thing. It
was underneath me. It was going to burst
out of the water any second and swallow
me whole.

I braced myself for the massive chomp to come and thought about all the awesome waves I'd caught in my life and all the awesome ones I'd never catch.

But nothing happened.

Until the fin popped up right in front of me once again.

Maybe it's not a shark at all, I thought. *Maybe it's just a playful bottlenose dolphin with an abnormally large fin.*

Then the animal's head popped out of the water.

'Hello, little surfer girl. Unfortunately for you I'm not a playful bottlenose

dolphin with an abnormally large fin. I'm actually a great white shark. You may have seen me in terrifying films like *Jaws* and *Sharknado*.'

The shark smiled at me, flashing his giant, great-white teeth. I stared into his awful, dead-black eyes, then his head disappeared below the surface.

Yep, it was a shark all right. I was trapped. I was doomed. I was about to become the latest gourmet delight on the hit reality cooking show *Master Shark*.

Unless . . .

I knew I couldn't possibly out-paddle him. But maybe . . . Maybe I could out-surf him. All I needed was the right wave.

I looked behind me. The perfect set

that had been rolling in only minutes earlier had suddenly become a soft, green lump of sea. It was flat as.

Great timing, ocean. Really great.

I rolled over a tiny little wave. Then another. And another. And nervously watched the fin circle my board, getting closer and closer.

Then I saw it. Rising like the main sail on a tall ship. The perfect wave. If I timed it right, I could catch it all the way to the shore before the shark even noticed.

I made two quick paddles forward then pushed myself up on my board, leaning in on the rails to control my direction just as the wave arrived.

I hit the crest and dropped down the face then sprang to my feet as the wave began to break.

I did it! I was on the wave! But when I looked back, Mr Chompy was right behind me. He wasn't giving up his breakfast so easily. He was riding the wave just like I was. And he had a big grin on his face. He was enjoying himself.

So here I am, catching the greatest wave of my short life, with a great white shark surfing behind me.

I *have* to out-surf him.

I glide through the barrel of the wave. All around me is a wall of green sea, and I need to find my way through it before it closes in on me. Maybe I can lose the shark in the backwash.

I stay low on the face of the wave, bending my knees to stay compact and keeping my chest face-forward to increase my speed and help me move in the right direction.

I spot the exit. It's like an open window to freedom. I burst out the end of the crystal tube . . . But the shark is still behind me.

This time he's snapping his jaws.
'Here I come,' he says. 'Om nom nom!'

I cut back towards the shore but
the great white turns with me. He's
right alongside me now, his fin cutting
through the foam like a samurai sword.

What's worse is that I can feel the
wave dying beneath me. The beach is still
so far away. I'm not going to make it.

The shark makes a lunge for me, but
I turn back hard on my left and cross
behind him.

'Tricky!' he says, and dives down
below me.

I see his large shadow in front of me.
His fin surfaces and I realise that this
is it.

The shark's massive jaws burst out of the water. 'Here's Chompy!' he says.

There's only one thing to do when a great white is trying to eat you. Ram something that isn't you down his throat. But all I have is my brand-new custom-made board with the killer rails and the awesome lightning bolt right down the centre.

So I reach down and rip off my leg rope, pitch my legs forward and launch the nose of my beautiful board straight at the shark, screaming, 'Eat this, Mr Chompy!'

The shark snaps the board in two as I dive into the air . . .

He swings back around and I land right on top of him, my feet on each side of his fin. Holy cow! I'm surfing on a shark!

I bend low to keep my balance and hope he doesn't dive back down under the water. He doesn't. Instead, he dips his head so that I slip down onto his nose.

'Om nom nom.' His delighted voice bubbles up through the water.

I know what he's planning. I've seen it in the movies. He's going toss me into the air, then open up those big jaws of his and gulp me down whole like a sardine.

But I can see something he can't.

I balance on the tip of his nose and get ready. He flips me up off his nose and I leap forward.

CRASH!

The shark slams into the sand bank as I somersault through the air and land on the beach on both feet. A perfect dismount.

I raise my hands with a flourish then take a bow as the shark shakes his big fat head and swims groggily away.

The judges hold up their scores.

10, 10, 10 and 9.5? Bit stingy, Judge Four!

I make sure to thank the shark when they hand me the trophy.

Well, what else did you expect? I told you I was good.

THE RALLY

BRRRING!

It was the recess bell. Kevin Lam
bolted out the classroom door clutching
his tennis ball. He sprinted to the
playground. Yes! He wasn't too late –
there was still one handball court left!

But running at full steam from the
other side of the quadrangle was Carlo
Santiago, the best handballer at Green
Hill Primary School.

Each boy leapt through the air and landed on the court at exactly the same time. 'Mine!' they both shouted.

'It's mine! I got here first,' said Carlo.

'No way! It's mine!' yelled Kevin.

It was a handball-court stand-off, and neither of the boys would back down.

A few moments later Kevin and Carlo's friends arrived and the stand-off turned into a shouting match between the two groups.

'Let's play for it!' suggested Kevin's best friend Tony, shouting over all the noise.

'Deal. First point wins. Winner gets the court,' said Carlo, '*for the whole week.*'

'Fine with us,' said Tony.

'You serve,' said Carlo to Kevin.

Kevin's face turned milk-white.

'I'm playing for our group,' said Tony.

'No way,' said Carlo. He pointed to Kevin. 'He ran for the court, he plays for the court.'

'Fine,' said Tony.

'Are you crazy?' whispered Kevin. 'I can't beat Carlo.'

'Sure you can.'

Kevin slapped his hand to his head in despair. Not only were they about to lose the court for the whole week, Carlo was about to humiliate him in front of all his friends. He looked up at Carlo, who was grinning in anticipation. He had beady, black shark's eyes and he played like a shark, too. His reflexes were lightning fast and he was the master of the deathblow – the single shot that could take out any opponent.

Kevin, on the other hand, was the master of the miss-hit. He was no match for Carlo, and Carlo knew it.

'Hurry up and serve, Lam,' said Carlo, tossing him the ball. 'We want our court.'

Kevin nervously gripped the ball, wondering where he could serve it so that it might give him a fighting chance. In the end he decided it didn't matter since he was going to lose anyway, and he served it straight down the middle.

Carlo waited for the ball to drop low so he could flick it into the corner of Kevin's square, but Kevin was at least half-ready for that shot. He played it back timidly to Carlo's right and prepared himself for Carlo's return.

'Too easy,' said Carlo. He smashed the ball deep into Kevin's court. It was all over before it had even started.

Except . . .

Somehow Kevin got to the ball. He lunged deep and raked it back behind him. It bounced over Carlo's head and landed in the back of his square. Now Carlo was on the run.

'Nice one, Kev!' shouted Tony.

Carlo slapped the ball back but Kevin was ready. He fired a shot at the right corner of Carlo's square.

'*Oooh*,' groaned the onlookers from both groups – which brought more kids over to watch.

Carlo didn't flinch. 'All right, time to get serious . . . *deadly* serious.'

He again allowed Kevin's return shot to drop until it almost reached the ground, then he smashed the ball

hard and low along
the ground. It was
unhittable.

But Kevin
lunged at the
ball. By some miracle, he got his hand to
it, bouncing it up off the concrete and
into Carlo's square.

'What? How . . . ?' But Carlo couldn't
say anything else – he had to sprint to
get to the ball before the second bounce.

Kevin couldn't believe it. He'd never
returned a ball that low before. He must
have got lucky . . . That was it! His lucky
ball!

It was the first time Kevin had ever
played with his ball at school. He had

only brought it in today because Tony had lost his on the way home from school yesterday, bouncing it too close to a stormwater drain.

Kevin had never really believed in his lucky ball before. It was just something he told his little sister.

'Why do you always win, Kevin?' she would ask.

'This is my lucky ball. I never lose with my lucky ball.'

Well, it used to be just something he said to his sister, but now that Kevin thought about it, it was true. He had never lost with this ball. Whether he was playing his sister, the kid from next door or his cousins who came to stay in the holidays, Kevin always won. Sure, all those kids were a lot younger than he was, but maybe that didn't matter. Maybe it *was* the ball. How else could he have faced off against the best handballer in the school and survived this long?

With every shot he returned, Kevin only became more convinced. His lucky tennis ball was helping him beat Carlo Santiago.

He looked around and was startled to see so many kids watching. Where had they all come from?

Tony started a commentary of all the action along with a tall, brown-haired sixth grader whose friends had stopped to watch the game.

'Well, this *is* a surprise, Gloria!' said Tony. 'Just when you thought our current champion, Carlo Santiago, had things all wrapped up, newcomer Kevin Lam steps up and plays one of the all-time greatest returns.'

'That's right, Tony,' said Gloria. 'This rally has been going for seven minutes now –'

What? Seven minutes! Kevin couldn't believe it!

'– and there's such a buzz in the crowd. They all want to know just who will win the point!'

'Yes, Gloria, and let's not forget what they're playing for. The winner will have exclusive court rights for a whole week.

It's no wonder it's getting tense out there!'

'Is it possible, Tony, that we might even see them break the record for longest handball rally ever?'

'Well, that would be something. As you know, no rally has ever lasted till the end of recess before.'

'Yes, but how long can this plucky challenger hold out against the master of the deathblow?' mused Gloria.

The minutes ticked by and both boys battled on. Their palms glowed red. Their fingertips went numb. But they didn't stop. Not for a second. Kevin was starting to believe he could actually win. With every shot the crowd roared and

Kevin's confidence grew, thanks to his lucky ball.

'Well, the champ's tried everything,' said Tony, 'and I mean *everything*. He's pulled out every trick shot he knows – between the legs, over the shoulder, the up and under, the lob, the push, the pat, the corkscrew, the cobra, the hammer – and *nothing's* worked. How is that possible, Gloria?'

'Who knows, Tony? But Kevin Lam is really gaining support from the crowd, now. They want to see him take this all the way to the bell!'

'Just 30 seconds left!' exclaimed Tony. 'This could be a new record, folks!'

SLAP.

WHAP.

SMASH.

'Twenty seconds!'

The crowd began the countdown.

'. . . 18, 17, 16 . . .'

Carlo slammed the ball hard into the corner.

Kevin stumbled but dragged it back before losing his balance.

'. . . 13, 12, 11 . . .'

'Lam just needs to hang in there!' cried Tony. 'Can he do it?'

But then Kevin saw something in Carlo's eyes and knew that this was it. This was Carlo's last chance to use the deathblow.

'. . . Ten, nine, eight . . .'

Carlo flicked the ball out of his wrist. It flew low and fast into the opposite corner of Kevin's square.

'. . . Seven, six, five . . .'

It took all of Kevin's speed and strength to dive for the ball.

'. . . Four, three, two . . .'

He just got his fingers to it as he hit the ground.

The ball bounced high into the air . . .

'One!'

And landed just inside the line.

BRRRING!

'He's done it!' yelled Tony. 'Kevin Lam has won the point *and* the court for the whole week *and* he's smashed the record for the longest rally in the history of handball! Gloria is with him now . . .'

'Well, Kevin, that was truly amazing! Tell us: what was it that allowed you to keep returning those shots?'

'I guess I owe it all to my lucky tennis ball,' said Kevin, holding it up proudly for all to see. 'Hold on,' he said, looking at the ball more closely. The initials 'CS' were clearly printed on the side. 'This isn't my ball, it's Carlo's.'

But no one heard. Tony, the brown-haired year-six girl and everyone else were heading back to class.

'Guess I've got myself a new lucky ball,' said Kevin to himself. And with that, the new handball champion of the school headed off to class.

THE SPOON

'I can't believe we lost again!' sighed Kyle as he slumped into the passenger seat of his dad's ute. 'That's six games in a row, now.'

'Well, at least it was closer this week,' said Kyle's dad, reversing out of the carpark of the Redville Rams Junior Rugby League Club.

'It was 44 to four!' exclaimed Kyle.

'At this rate we'll get the wooden spoon for sure.'

'Could be worse,' said his dad as they sped down the main road towards a large, dark storm cloud.

'How?' asked Kyle.

'Well . . .'

Keeping his eyes on the road, his dad reached over to the glove compartment and fumbled through the mess of yellowing road maps, half-empty biros and rock-hard Minties. Finally he pulled out an old, greasy wooden spoon.

'Ah! Knew it was in there somewhere!'

'Ew! What *is* that?' said Kyle.

'What does it look like? It's a wooden spoon. In my day, if your team came last, they really gave you one. They gave it to me because I was the captain, back when I played for the Wangarella Wombats. That year our team lost six of our best players. All their dads were farmers who sold up because of the drought. In the first game of the season we got thumped 88 to nil.'

'Eighty-eight to nil?' gasped Kyle.

'Yep. You think losing six in a row is bad? Try 14.'

'So you got a real wooden spoon. Big deal. How's that worse?'

'Well, it wasn't just about coming last. There was the curse, as well,' said Kyle's dad gravely.

'Curse?' repeated Kyle, blinking.

'The curse of the wooden spoon,' said his father. 'Every year the town that won the wooden spoon suffered a terrible catastrophe. It started when Mullimdilli won the spoon. The next week the town's pub burnt down. Each year was the same for whoever won the spoon: floods, bushfires, mouse plagues, locusts, headlice . . . One year Culumburra won the spoon and their mayor was struck by lightning when he was out on the golf course.'

Almost on cue, a rumble of thunder sounded in the distance. Kyle looked around nervously as the sky darkened.

His father raised an eyebrow and continued with his story. 'In 20 years, Wangarella had never won the wooden spoon so never felt the sting of the curse. But that year, because the team sat at the bottom of the ladder, the whole town became nervous. You couldn't walk down Main Street without someone calling out, "You boys better win a game. We don't want the curse!"'

'People actually said that?'

'Yep. Especially this one very annoying girl with pigtails. We called her Loudmouth Lizzie. She was the toughest girl in Wangarella and everyone was scared of her, even our coach. She was there at every game we played, yelling abuse from the sidelines . . . which really didn't help at all.'

Kyle's dad stopped talking and watched a few fat raindrops splatter on the windscreen.

'So what happened?' asked Kyle.

'Well, it came down to the last round and we were up against the Bartley Brumbies. Their side had lost a lot of players that season as well.'

'Drought?' asked Kyle.

'Nope. German measles. Went through half the team. But on the last round they were back to full strength.

Luckily, we'd managed to get some players from the age group below to help us make up the numbers but we were still one player short of a full team. To make things worse, the drought chose that exact moment to break. As we ran onto the field, the sky went black with rain clouds.'

Kyle gulped.

'We were lining up for kick-off, wishing we at least had a full team, when another Wangarella player came jogging out of the change sheds to make up the 13. You wouldn't believe who it was!'

'Who?' asked Kyle.

'Loudmouth Lizzie.'

'What?'

'Yep. No one recognised her at first because she'd shaved off her pigtails and borrowed some shoulder pads from her brother. With the Wombats jersey on and the crew cut, she looked like one of the toughest Wangarella players to ever take the field. Even the ref didn't suspect a thing. For the first time that season, we had 13 players.'

'Then what happened?' asked a riveted Kyle.

'Well, the rain, that's what happened. Right from the kick-off it bucketed down. The footy field turned into a mud bath. You could barely run without one of your boots getting sucked right off your foot. But that didn't stop us trying.

'The score was nil all for most of the first 40. Then right before the half-time siren, Bartley put up the bomb and got a rebound off the goal post. One of their forwards caught it and flopped over the try-line to score. They converted the try and it was six to nil.

'At half-time we stood around in the change sheds, wiping the mud from our faces and listening to Coach Peters talk strategy. All of us, even Coach, tried to ignore the fact that there was a girl standing in the change room. Finally, someone decided to say something. Of course that someone was Loudmouth Lizzie.

'"You could try passing the ball to me for a change!" she said.

'"But you're . . . a girl!" said our lock Brad.

'"So?" said Lizzie. "I'm the best player out there!"

'No one said anything after that. We all knew Lizzie had a point. I decided that if I got the chance, I'd pass her the ball.

'The second half was the same as the first. Pouring rain, a mile of mud and 25 boys and one girl battling it out for second-last place. By then the field had become a complete and utter bog. We couldn't get anywhere with the ball. As soon as we ran forward we'd slip over in the mud.

'With just five minutes on the clock, I grabbed the ball from the dummy half and weighed up my options. A bomb? A chip kick? A grubber?

'That's when I heard it coming towards me – a low, terrible growl. It was Lizzie. She was steaming in, her eyes blazing like red coals. I didn't hesitate for a second. I passed her the ball, then stood back and watched her go.

'Lizzie charged to the line where the Bartley players were crouched down, ready to defend, and vaulted high into the air. Apparently the five years of ballet

lessons her mother had forced her to take to make her more ladylike hadn't been a total waste of money after all. Lizzie leapt over the line of Bartley players and scored right under the black dot.

'We rushed in to congratulate Lizzie, most of us slipping straight over in the mud. But we couldn't celebrate for long. There were just two minutes left and the score was six to four.

'I converted the goal to make it six all, then rushed back to our half, ready to receive the kick-off. We had less than a minute to get to the other end of the field and try for a field goal.

'Once again it was Lizzie who stepped up to take the ball. It was one of the best runs from a forward I've ever seen. Lizzie didn't seem to feel the mud or the rain or the other players. She burst through the defence like a comet through the night sky. By the fifth tackle we were at the halfway line with less than ten seconds left on the clock. I knew halfway would have to be close enough.

'I moved back into position and waited for the ball. With just a split second to line up the posts, I booted that ball as hard I could.'

The rain began pelting down even harder and Kyle's dad pulled over for a moment. It was simply too heavy to continue. Kyle squirmed in his seat.

He looked up at his dad. 'Well?'

'I got it. The ball sailed straight through the posts right on the siren. Everyone went wild. We'd won our first game of the season.'

'Hang on. If Wangarella won, how did you get this?' asked Kyle, waving the wooden spoon.

'Well, it didn't take too long for the truth to come out,' said his dad. 'About a week later we were stripped of our two competition points for winning the game and I was presented with the spoon.'

'You lost your points just because one of your players was a girl?' asked Kyle.

'No, we lost the points because we had played with an unregistered player.'

'What about the curse? Did something bad happen to the town?'

'Yep. That year at the town fair, the Ferris wheel broke down for two hours.'

'That's all?' asked Kyle.

'Well, it was very inconvenient, son.'

'And what about Loudmouth Lizzie? What happened to her?'

'Funnily enough, Lizzie and I became quite close after the game. She wasn't that loud or annoying when you got to know her. Ten years later, Elizabeth Barnes and I got married.'

'What? You mean Mum is Loudmouth Lizzie?'

'Yep. Where do you think you get your competitive streak from?'

Kyle sat there, stunned.

'Rain's stopped,' said his dad, pulling the ute back onto the road.

And as they drove away towards a small ray of sunlight that was poking through the grey sky, Kyle's father turned and smiled. 'You see, sometimes, Kyle, even when you lose, you win.'

WHEELS OF FORTUNE

'Here comes Max McKenzie! He's hit that final set of doubles[1] at warp speed. Now he's round the last berm[2] and into the straight, manualling[3] all the way to

---

1   By the way, a double is two jumps close together.
2   Oh, and a berm is a curved slope on a track.
3   Manualling is popping a wheelie without pedalling. Don't know what a wheelie is? Google it. I'm busy writing this!

the finish line. What a performance from the young rider!' called the race commentator.

'Nice going, little bro,' said his twin sister Amy when Max emerged from the rider's area of the National BMX Supercross Championships.

'Amy, I'm not your little bro! I'm taller than you!' said Max defensively.

'Yeah, but you're younger.'

'By seven minutes,' said Max, rolling his eyes.

'Stop whining,' said Amy. 'Let's go check out the trophy again.'

Amy and Max sprinted over to the media tent and ducked inside. Encased in a large glass cabinet was a life-size

BMX not that different to the one Max had just been riding, except that it was completely gold. Gold rims, gold tuffs, gold pedals, gold chain. Even the frame was a special gold and carbon fibre alloy.

'Wow,' said Max with a whistle. 'There she is. The golden Mongoose.'

'You say that as if it's not the third time you've been in here today!' said Amy.

The bike was the prize for the winner of the championships. The unusual trophy was to be awarded to the most outstanding rider of the tournament.

'What would you even do with a bike like that? It's not as if you could actually ride it around anywhere,' said Amy.

'I wouldn't need to ride it. I'd just sit on it and bask in its golden glory,' said Max.

'That reminds me. I've got my heat in three minutes!' cried Amy. 'Thanks for making me late,' she said, thumping Max on the arm before disappearing out of the media tent in a blur.

———

'Are you sure you left them in there?' whined Max later that afternoon as he stood in front of the locked gate in the fading light. 'Mum and Dad will kill us if they realise we've snuck out just to find your lucky gloves.'

'But I need them. You know I can't race without them!'

'Well, the place is locked. Let's come back tomorrow,' said Max.

'Stop being a chicken. Let's just ask a security guard to let us in,' said Amy.

But before they could look for one, they heard a whirring noise above their heads.

They peered through the darkness. 'Looks like some kind of drone,' said

Max. 'It's heading towards the media tent.'

Sure enough, the drone hovered over the media tent then lowered a long cable that hooked the top of the tent, lifted it off the ground, swung it to the side, then put it back down. A moment later, the cable hooked itself onto something else: the glass cabinet with the golden Mongoose inside. The drone rose into the air and carried the cabinet off into the dusk.

'What?' gasped Max. 'Did they just steal the whole display case?'

'We have to stop them!' cried Amy.

'To the bikes!' Max said.

Moments later, Max and Amy were

pedalling hard after the drone. It wasn't that difficult to follow. The drone had to move slowly because of its load, so it was easy to keep up with.

They tracked the drone to an old abandoned warehouse, just outside the city. The twins hid behind a dumpster and watched as a mysterious figure wearing a black BMX suit, helmet and face mask, worked a remote that controlled the drone. The man gently landed the display case in the rubbish-strewn carpark of the warehouse and hurried over to pry open the glass door. A moment later, he was pedalling the golden Mongoose out and cackling to himself with glee.

'He's gonna ride it away,' said Amy.

'Not if we stop him first!'

Max tore off after the Rider in Black and Amy followed.

'He's heading into the city!' called Max.

The twins pedalled harder but the Rider in Black was skilled. He was bunny-hopping off gutters and manualling over hills as well as anyone Max had ever seen.

'This dude can ride!' shouted Amy over the peak-hour traffic.

The Rider in Black cut through a park, gliding down a set of stairs with a perfect double peg grind[4] on the rail. Not to be outdone, Max and Amy followed with simultaneous double peg grinds on opposite stair rails.

The Rider in Black glanced back to see Amy and Max in hot pursuit and from that point on it wasn't just a chase. It was a freestyle shred fest.

The Rider in Black tail whipped[5] off the edge of a fountain and Max and Amy

---

4   An amazing trick where you slide along using the pegs attached to the axle. I suggest YouTube-ing a clip.

5   A tail whip is when you spin the whole bike (the frame and the back wheel) over the front wheel.

did the same. Then he pulled a 180 off a park bench followed by a fakie,[6] spinning his golden ride around after a long hard glare at Max, who followed him with his own 180 and fakie. Amy, who was a natural at freestyling, flew over the top with an amazing 360.

The three riders burst back onto the street, weaving in and out of traffic.

Max's legs were burning but he wasn't about to give up the chase now. He got within an arm's length of the golden Mongoose, but a delivery truck cut him off.

---

6   A fakie is another cool trick where you quickly change direction.

He turned back to warn his sister but before he could yell out he watched her bounce her bike off a parked car and somersault over the top of the truck, landing on the other side of the road in front of the Rider in Black, cutting him off.

'Sick aerial, sis!' yelled Max.

The crook took a sharp right and Max and Amy went after him. They were barrelling down a steep road that ended in a dead end at Circular Quay.

'We've got him now,' said Amy.

'Give it up, dude!' Max called as they sped down towards the wharf. But then he noticed a whole bus load of tourists snapping photos of the Harbour Bridge.

Max and Amy were heading straight for them, at high speed!

'Outta the way!' called Max.

The tourists scrambled aside as the riders hurtled towards them. Max and Amy dodged in between the tourists, trying to keep track of the Rider in Black, but when the crowd cleared, they realised he'd slammed on his brakes right in front of them.

'Look out!' cried Max.

But it was too late. He tried to swerve out of the way and smashed straight into his sister. Both he and Amy went flying over the end of the pier in a spectacular flip.

SPLASH!

As Amy and Max sank slowly with their bikes to the bottom of the harbour, the Rider in Black cackled evilly above them.

'You lose!' he said.

Then everything went black.

'GAME OVER' read the wide-screen TV in Max and Amy's living room.

'Good one, Max!' groaned Amy. 'We almost had him that time!'

'Sorry, sis, my thumb slipped on the controller,' said Max. 'Play again?'

'You're on!' said Amy.

Max smiled. The pouring rain outside meant they couldn't ride their real BMX bikes around the neighbourhood like they'd planned to, but playing the video game he'd got for his birthday was the next best thing.

Max clicked on 'CONTINUE'.

'Ready?'

'Ready,' said Amy. 'But this time, let me lead. I'm the oldest, after all.'

'By seven minutes!' said Max.

'Stop whining,' said Amy.

Before Max could complain, the game had started.

'Here comes Amy McKenzie! She's hit that final set of doubles at warp speed. Now she's round the last berm and into the straight, manualling all the way to the finish line. What a performance from the young rider!'

MARCO'S MAGIC GLOVES

THUD!

The ball struck the back of the net and Marco Marcino dropped his head in shame. Another goal had slipped past his gloves. Marco was officially having his worst season ever and so was his team, the Littleton Llamas. They'd just lost their third game in a row and even though his teammates never said anything, Marco knew what they were thinking. It was all because of his terrible goalkeeping.

As he walked home after the game, Marco wondered how things had become so bad. He just didn't seem to be able to anticipate which way to dive. Whenever he went one way, the striker always kicked the ball the other. He couldn't get it right.

'I can help you,' called a voice from behind him.

Marco sprang around and saw an old man shuffling towards him.

'I'm not allowed to talk to strangers!' said Marco. But the truth was that Marco recognised the old man from the game.

Marco remembered him because he had been watching silently but intently from the sidelines and he wore a strange, old-fashioned brown suit and hat.

'Don't worry, Marco, we're not really strangers,' said the old man as he got closer. 'I used to know your grandfather, Mario Marcino, a long time ago.'

'You knew my grandfather?' asked Marco. His grandfather had passed away when Marco had been just three years old.

'Oh yes! We lived in the same village in Naples,' said the old man in his thick Italian accent. 'In fact, we played on the same team: Club Napolitano. He was one of the greatest goalkeepers I've ever seen.'

'I never knew Nonno Mario was a goalkeeper,' said Marco.

'He was, and I have something of his that might help you improve your game.'

The old man reached inside his suit jacket and pulled out a pair of battered brown leather goalie's gloves. They were unlike any Marco had ever seen before.

'These gloves are very special. They weren't just your grandfather's. They were passed down from goalkeeper to goalkeeper in Club Napolitano. Some of those players went on to keep for team Italia!' said the old man.

'They smell,' said Marco, screwing up his nose.

'Of course they smell! They have the sweat of 20 champions in them. That's what gives them their magic!'

'Magic?' asked Marco.

'Yes, magic,' said the old man, his blue eyes twinkling like Christmas-tree lights. 'Wear these gloves and you'll never miss a ball.'

'Wow! Thank you,' said Marco, looking down at the gloves in awe.

'But be careful. They're very powerful. Never wear them after the final whistle or there may be side effects.'

'Okay,' said Marco, still staring down at the gloves. 'What sort of side effects?'

But when he looked up the old man had gone.

All through the next week Marco couldn't wait for the game. Finally the day came. When he pulled on his grandfather's old gloves they seemed to tighten around his hands, as if they were shrinking down for a custom fit. They may have looked old and outdated, but they felt stronger and lighter than his normal gloves. Marco had his doubts that the gloves would make any difference to the way he played, but he didn't think they could make him play any worse than he had been.

Still, he never expected anything like what happened when he went to make his first save of the game.

As the opposition striker ran towards him, his hands began to tingle, his gloves began to twitch and Marco suddenly heard a boy's voice inside his head.

'*A sinistra*,' the voice said. Luckily Marco's mother had taught him some basic Italian. It meant 'On the left side.'

The striker took his shot, booting the ball across the goal face, and Marco responded quickly, diving to his left and catching the ball cleanly.

'Great save, Marco,' called one of his Llamas teammates.

A few minutes later, the opposition had another chance at goal. His hands began to tingle again. '*A destra*,' said the voice.

The right side, thought Marco.

As the opposition centre took his shot, Marco moved a few steps to his right and dived.

Another perfect save.

It went on like that all game. No one could get the ball past Marco's magic gloves. And the next week was just the same.

'Marco,' said one of his teammates after the game, 'how did you get so good all of a sudden?'

Marco shrugged. 'Must be my magic gloves,' he joked.

'Magic gloves! Good one!'

Marco smiled, but felt a little stab of guilt. It was almost too easy.

As each game went by, Marco's goal-saving record kept on improving. His coach kept raving about him.

'In all my years of coaching I've never seen anyone anticipate the way you do, Marco!' said his coach after their sixth straight win.

'I'm just lucky, I guess,' said Marco sheepishly, as he shoved his grandfather's gloves into his backpack. He still remembered what the old man had told him and never kept the gloves on after the final whistle.

'Lucky? Six straight games without conceding a goal isn't luck. It's amazing! Keep this up and we're a shoo-in for the final.'

Marco's coach was right. Soon the Littleton Llamas were one win away from making it to the final.

But after another great performance by Marco and his team in the semifinal, something unexpected happened. In the dying minutes of the game, Marco lunged to his right to make another great save and accidentally bumped his head on the goalpost, knocking himself out.

When he came to, the game was over and his coach was standing over him.

'You okay, Marco?'

Marco nodded groggily. It took a moment for him to realise that he was still wearing his gloves. He struggled to sit up and started pulling them off – but they wouldn't budge.

Come on! he thought. But it was no use. His gloves were stuck to his hands as if they'd been glued on with superglue.

Okay, he thought, *don't panic. I'll just have to get them off at home.* But as he hurried home, he couldn't help wondering just what the old man had meant by 'side effects'.

When he arrived home, Marco didn't know what to do. *Should I cut them off?* He wondered. *If I do that, I won't be able to wear them in the final. But I can't keep them on all week . . .*

He had no choice. He had to cut them off.

Marco picked up his scissors, but his hand dropped them immediately. He picked them up again, and his hand threw them out his bedroom window.

The gloves don't want to come off!

Marco was right. They had taken over. For the whole week, Marco had to hide his gloved hands from everyone to avoid awkward questions about why he was wearing them. To make matters worse, the gloves were now in complete control of his hands. They decided what he did and didn't do. For example, they did like eating his mother's spaghetti but they didn't like doing homework. Marco got detention after detention for not having his work done.

When the day of the grand final arrived, Marco was relieved. At least he could put the gloves to good use after all the trouble they'd caused him that week. But when Marco stood in the goal area ready to make his first save against the Pennsville Pythons, it wasn't just one voice he heard anymore. It was 20. Every past champion goalie from Club Napolitano was yelling instructions in his head.

'*A sinistra,*' said one.

'*No, alla destra, stupido!*' called another.

'*Che asurdita! Al centro!*' said a third.

Marco couldn't keep up with all the voices.

THUD!

The ball hit the back of the net and the Llamas fans went silent. Marco had let in a goal.

His teammates were stunned for a moment but somehow they steeled themselves and managed to even the score. It was all locked up at 1–1 but Marco knew it was only a matter of time before the Pythons tried again.

They got their chance early in the second half when a Littleton defender gave away a penalty right in front of the box.

The voices started arguing with each other again as the Pythons player lined up his penalty kick. It was so noisy Marco couldn't think at all. He couldn't take it anymore.

'Shut up!' he screamed. 'I can do this by myself!'

Suddenly the voices in his head fell silent and the gloves on his hands loosened.

Marco stared hard at the Pythons player as he ran in to take his shot. He watched his every move for a sign. Then he noticed the direction of the player's gaze.

A sinistra, thought Marco. *He's going left.*

Sure enough, the Pythons player fired the ball to the left corner.

Marco was there to stop it. No goal! Marco couldn't believe it. He'd made his save without any help at all!

For the last 20 minutes of the match, Marco saved three more goals and then, in the dying minutes, his teammates finally scored a goal of their own.

The whistle went. The Littleton Llamas had won the grand final!

His teammates ran around the field, cheering and pulling their jerseys up over their heads in celebration. But Marco was busy searching the crowd for a certain familiar face. Finally Marco spotted him, still wearing his old brown suit and hat. Marco waved to the old man who smiled, his blue eyes twinkling brighter than ever.

———

Later that night Marco found himself thumbing through his parents' old photo albums. But he couldn't find what he was looking for.

'Mum,' he asked, 'do we have any photos of Nonno Mario before he died?'

'Let me see,' said his mum. 'Yes, here's one of the last ones we took of

Mario. He loved that old brown suit. It's the one we buried him in.'

Marco looked into his grandfather's twinkling blue eyes and sighed. *Thank you, Nonno.*

Prego, said a voice in his head, which in Italian means 'You're welcome.'

GAME ON

Rachel and Claudine stood toe to toe
in the centre of the netball court, eyes
locked and teeth bared. It was the Under
Tens Green Hill district grand final. This
game was as serious as it gets.

'We're gonna thrash you!' growled
Rachel. 'Hope your coach hasn't got
any plans after the game because she's
going to be picking your bones up off

the court, one by one!'

'That's funny. I was wondering if *your* coach had plans after the game 'cause *we're* going to smash *you* into tiny pieces, then we're gonna step on all those tiny pieces and grind them into the concrete. Your coach is going to need a broom to sweep away the dust when we're finished with you!' snarled Claudine.

'Oh yeah?' said Rachel.

'Yeah!' said Claudine.

Rachel glared at Claudine. Claudine glared back.

To the crowd it looked as if World War Three was about to erupt in the centre of the court. They would never have suspected that Claudine and Rachel were in fact bffs – and had been since kindergarten. They did everything together. Everything, that is, except play netball. Claudine lived on the north side of Green Hill so she played for the North Green Hill Rainbows. Rachel lived on the south side so she played for the South Green Hill Unicorns. Both girls were razor-sharp Goal Shooters and team captains and had been dreaming about a grand-final victory since they started playing netball four years ago.

Today was the day. Both girls were determined to win the game, no matter what it took.

The umpire tossed the coin. 'Rainbows captain: your call.'

'Tails never fails!' said Claudine.

'Tails,' said the umpire. 'Rainbows captain: your choice. Do you want to pick the side you goal or start with the ball?'

'We'll start with the ball, thanks,' said Claudine.

The umpire handed the ball to the Rainbows' Centre and blew the whistle. Game on.

The Rainbows worked the ball quickly around the court – from Centre to Wing Attack to Goal Attack till finally Claudine

had the ball. The Unicorns Goal Keeper
was right up in her face but Claudine
didn't flinch. She took a single step
closer to the goal and, with the grace and
poise of a flamingo, balanced on one leg
and popped the ball up in the air.

Swish!

It dropped through the hoop without
even touching the ring.

1–0.

The Unicorns got their chance to
even the score at the next centre pass.

'Quick hands, girls!' called Rachel.

The Unicorns listened to their captain,
working the ball quickly down the court.

'Come on, Rainbows! Defend!' cried
Claudine.

But a high lob pass from the Unicorns Goal Attack sent the ball straight into Rachel's waiting hands. She took the shot before the Rainbows Goal Keeper could react.

Boing! It bounced off the ring.

Undeterred, Rachel leapt up over the head of the Rainbows Goal Defence and grabbed it back. She steadied herself then coolly tossed the ball through the hoop.

1–1.

The ball went back and forth and so did the score. When the Rainbows got a goal, the Unicorns struck back. When the Unicorns managed to intercept a pass or foil a shooting

opportunity, the Rainbows tightened
their defence and did the same. The
scores stayed locked up. Two all.
Three all. Four all.

After the first quarter it was five all.

At half-time it was 12 all.

'Come on, Rainbows, we need to be
quicker in defence. They're all over us!'
said Claudine to her team.

'Watch your passes, Unicorns. We
can't let them take the lead!' said Rachel
to her team.

'This is it. This is what we worked
towards all year . . .' said Claudine.

'This is it. Eyes on the prize. We've
got this . . .' said Rachel.

'One more half . . .' said Claudine.

'One more half . . .' said Rachel.

'Give it everything you've got!' said both girls.

When the teams took to the court for the second half of the game, there was a fiery spark in the eyes of every player. The crowd had already seen a good game, but what they saw next amazed them. The passes got faster. The running got quicker. The blocking got stronger. Each girl on the court was playing the game of her life.

But it was the shooting that stunned the crowd most of all. Rachel and Claudine never missed a shot. They matched each other goal for goal and, when the whistle blew for the end of the third quarter, the score was still locked up at 20 goals each.

The teams gathered for the three-minute break. Each of the girls was exhausted. Every face was flushed pink with heat. Sweat poured from their foreheads and steam rose from their bodies. But they couldn't wait to get back on court.

'Let's go, Rainbows, LET'S GO!' screamed Claudine's team.

'Unicorns, Unicorns, Unicorns, FIGHT!' screamed Rachel's team.

The final quarter started and the contest was as close as ever. Both teams fought for every pass and with every goal the tension grew. As the clock ticked down, the crowd grew more and more excited. Who would be in the lead when the final whistle blew?

And then, with just two minutes left till full-time, disaster struck the Unicorns. Rachel threw the ball up for a shot – and missed. What's worse, she missed catching the rebound, too. She stared in disbelief as the ball was snatched up by the Rainbows Goal Keeper.

The Rainbows worked the ball down to their goal circle, being particularly careful with their passes. Centre passed to Wing Defence. Wing Defence passed to Wing Attack. Wing Attack passed to Goal Attack, till finally Claudine had the ball. She lined up the shot carefully and popped the ball into the air.

Boing!

It hit the ring and bounced into the hands of the Unicorns Goal Keeper.

'Nooo!' screamed Claudine. 'Defend, Rainbows, defend!'

The Unicorns Goal Keeper passed to Wing Defence. Wing Defence passed to Centre . . . But there was no one for the Centre to pass to – each player was blocked.

What was she going to do? She had one more second until the umpire would pull her up for held ball! A moment later the Unicorns Centre saw a chance. She bounced the ball to Wing Attack, who tossed a long lob pass over everyone's heads to Rachel.

Rachel leapt up and caught it. When she landed, her feet were just inside the goal circle.

She was a long way from the goal ring. She took a step forward and balanced on one wobbly, nervous leg as Claudine and the rest of the Rainbows looked on in horror.

Rachel fired the ball at the goal.

It bounced once on the hoop then skidded around the rim three times. Every player and every spectator held their breath. Finally, the ball made up its mind and dropped through.

Goal!

The whistle blew for time and the Unicorns screamed. They'd won! They'd won their first grand final!

Claudine and her teammates hung their heads. Some slumped to the ground. Some stood and stared. They'd worked so hard. They'd come so close. They had it. Then it was stolen away.

'This isn't over,' said Claudine, as she stood in the centre of the court facing the winning captain. 'The Unicorns may have won this year, but the Rainbows will be back. Next year, you won't be so lucky!'

'Oh yeah?' said Rachel.

'Yeah!' said Claudine.

Rachel glared at Claudine. Claudine glared back.

Then both girls smiled.

'Good game,' said Rachel.

'Well played,' said Claudine. And right there in the middle of the court they hugged.

'So you wanna have a sleepover at my place tonight?' asked Rachel.

'Sure, I'll ask Mum,' said Claudine.

'We can do makeovers!' said Rachel.

'Cool! I'll bring my Bedazzler,' said Claudine.

The two girls walked off court arm in arm and, while it confused many of the spectators, there was no doubt in the minds of both the girls. They were bffs. And nothing, not even a grand final, could come between best friends.

At least, not until next year.

THE GHOST OF BARRY KEEN

Have you ever had one of those days that started off great and ended up awful? I mean, *really* awful. Change-your-name-and-move-to-another-town awful.

Well, I have.

It happened to me just last weekend. It was supposed to be the best day of my life. It was my very first game of AFL for the Everly Emus against our local rivals,

the Derrigal Dingos, so I got up early
and headed off with my dad and brother
Gary to Derrigal Oval. I was so excited
I needed to pee.

That's when things started to go
wrong.

'Dad, can we stop at a servo? I need
to go to the toilet,' I said.

'Why didn't you go before we left?'
said Dad. He always said that.

'I did. I need to go again.'

'Well, we'll be there soon. You'll just
have you hold it,' said Dad. He always
said that too.

'Hey Eric,' said Gary, 'I wouldn't be
using the change-room toilets if I were
you.'

'Why not?' I asked.

'Barry Keen will get you!' said Gary.

So then I went and asked the worst thing possible. 'Who's Barry Keen?'

Gary leaned over with a creepy glint in his eye. 'Barry Keen was one of Derrigal's all-time greatest players. He was a giant forward with a big red beard and an even bigger appetite. They say that Barry ate a dozen meat pies during every game.'

'Twelve pies a game?' It seemed a bit far-fetched to me.

'Three pies at the end of every quarter,' said Gary. 'But then one match, at three-quarter time, while Big Barry was polishing off his third pie, he choked on a piece of gristle and died right there on the side of the field. Now he haunts the dunnies in the visitors' sheds, scaring away the opponents of the Derrigal Dingos.'

Now I don't know if you have an older brother or not, but in case you don't, I'll let you know – they lie a lot. Sometimes, though, they manage to say something in a certain way so that even though you're sure it can't be true, you end up believing them anyway. That's what Gary did right at that moment. He made it sound true and I began to believe it.

So even though Dad said, 'Don't listen to him, Eric. That's just a stupid old urban legend,' I couldn't help believing Gary just a little.

And that's why things got even worse.

When we got to Derrigal Oval I joined up with the rest of my team. They were all practising kicks and marks and passes in the warm-up ground next to the oval.

I joined in the warm-ups but I just couldn't get Barry Keen off my mind. And I still needed to wee, worse than ever.

'Have you ever heard of Barry Keen?' I asked my teammate Kevin Long.

'Barry who?' asked Kevin.

Kevin had played with the Emus for two years. If he didn't know who Barry Keen was, then my brother had probably made it all up. I looked across at the visitors' sheds. They looked like ordinary change rooms to me.

A few minutes before the game was due to start I realised I didn't have a choice. I had to go find out for myself. The problem was I didn't want to go alone.

'Anyone need to go to the toilet?' I asked hopefully, but no one responded. I walked over to the change shed by myself and peeked inside.

'Hello?' I called.

There was no answer. The shed was empty. I took a few steps inside. It all seemed fine.

I walked over to an empty toilet stall and closed the door behind me.

Stupid, lying Gary, I thought as I lifted the lid of the toilet. But just as I was about to pee, I noticed something in the toilet bowl.

The water quivered and the reflection of a face appeared. The face of a man with a big red beard.

I couldn't move and I definitely couldn't wee. I couldn't even scream. Then I heard the creepiest noise all around me. It was coming up through the plumbing like a pipeline straight from hell. It was a low, gravelly voice singing slowly:

'I am the ghost of Barry Keen.

I am gruff and tough and mean.

Whosoever wants to wee,

He will have to first pay me . . .

THREE PIES.'

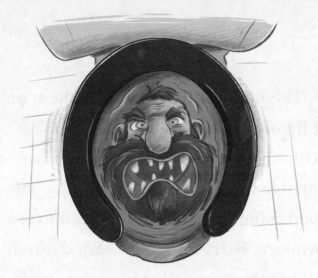

The toilet bowl started to bubble, then every toilet in the change sheds flushed at once.

I don't know how I made my legs move but I bolted out of there so quickly that I dropped my mouthguard on the change-room floor.

There was no way I was stopping to pick it up. I ran straight onto the oval, where my team was lining up for the game.

''Bout time,' said my coach.

The umpire balled it up for the start of the first quarter but I couldn't focus. I couldn't get Barry Keen's watery face or horrible voice out of my head. The only good thing was that I didn't need to wee anymore. Barry must have scared it right out of me.

I tried getting into the game but I didn't know what I was doing. At one point, someone handballed me a pass and I didn't even see it coming. It smacked me straight in the nose. The second quarter wasn't much better. When I finally got my first touch of the ball, I ran five metres and then booted the ball towards the opposition goals. One of the Dingos players took a great mark off my kick and scored a goal.

By half-time, we were down by four goals and three behinds and that urgent feeling had come back but there was no way I was going back in that change room, with or without pies for Barry. Instead, I tried to find a private place to have a wee, but I was out of luck. There were people everywhere.

We went back on for the third quarter and that feeling got worse and worse. I was really bursting now. Every time I went to make a tackle or chase down a kick, I could almost feel a little bit of wee coming out.

By the fourth quarter, things were critical. I was busting so badly it hurt. I was even starting to see things. When I looked out into the crowd, I didn't see the normal faces of the supporters. Instead I saw dozens of red-bearded Barry Keens. And they were all singing Barry's creepy song.

'We are the ghosts of Barry Keen
We are gruff and tough and mean.
If you are about to bust,
you will have to first pay us . . .
THREE PIES.'

Everywhere I looked everyone was eating pies. It was enough to make you sick!

I took to standing on the edge of the oval near the goal posts, to try to avoid the action and the crowd. I could hardly move. I was worried I was going to burst any second, right there in front of everyone. At least my teammates were doing okay without me. The scores were level now. We could even win it!

I just had to hold on a little longer.

I tried to clear my mind but I could still hear Barry's voice. It kept repeating like a broken record.

'Three pies. Three pies. Three pies.'

Then, with the clock down to just two minutes, the worst possible thing happened. Kevin Long kicked the ball straight to me and I somehow caught it.

'Quick, take the shot!' called Kevin.

I was standing right near the posts. I could kick the winning goal!

But then *it* would happen . . .

I didn't care. I had to take one for the team.

I lined the ball up and took the shot.

The ball sailed straight through the middle of the posts.

The small group of Emus supporters cheered.

The hooter sounded . . .

And nothing else happened. I hadn't wet my pants. It was a miracle!

My teammates rushed over and lifted me onto their shoulders. Even the coach joined in. 'Three cheers for Eric!' he shouted.

'Hip hip hooray!' everyone sang as they tossed me up into the air.

I tried to stop them.

'No!' I cried.

But it was too late.

Some teams pour Gatorade over their coach's head to celebrate a victory.

This was wet and sticky, but it wasn't Gatorade.

Wee went everywhere.

Now you know what I mean by awful. It doesn't get much worse than weeing on the heads of your teammates and coach in your first game of the season.

Afterwards, when we'd cleaned ourselves up a little, I tried to explain what happened but no one believed me. I said goodbye to my unimpressed teammates and Dad made Gary apologise for telling me the story about Barry Keen.

'I can't believe you fell for that rubbish,' said Gary, between bites of a meat pie that was dribbling down his chin. 'I'm sorry . . . Sorry, you're so stupid you believed me.'

'Well,' I said, looking as miserable as possible, 'maybe you could make it up to me by getting my mouthguard. I left it in the visitors' shed.'

'Still scared, little bro?' Gary laughed. 'Sure, whatever, I need to go anyway.'

He walked over to the shed and disappeared inside. It wasn't long before he came back out, only now he looked as white as a sheet.

'Are you okay, Gary?' I smiled. 'You look as if you've seen a ghost.'

'B-B-Barry,' he stammered. 'He's real and he's mean. He took my pie and now he wants two more.'

'Well, you better go get them for him. You don't want to keep Barry Keen waiting.'

Gary whimpered and then looked down. There was a little puddle forming on the ground below him.

Maybe things weren't all bad. At least I wasn't the only kid going home with wet shorts.

THE ETERNAL GAME

'Well, you're definitely dead,' said
the silver-haired man as he put his
stethoscope away.

'Dead?' asked Ben, stunned. The
last thing he remembered was sticking
his knife into the toaster after his toast
got stuck. Then everything went black.
Now he was in a small room that was
completely white. The walls, the door,
the floor. White everywhere.

'Yes, we just like to make sure,' said the man, smiling. 'Sometimes it doesn't take the first time.' He was wearing white and his teeth were so bright and clean he looked as if he'd just stepped out of a toothpaste ad.

'B-B-But . . . this can't be happening,' stammered Ben.

'I know! Exciting, isn't it?' said the white-toothed man pleasantly. 'I imagine you'll want to get started right away so I'll take you straight to the stadium.'

'Stadium?'

'That's right. You're our new centre forward. Come on, let's go meet the team.'

As the man turned around, Ben noticed a large pair of feathery white

wings sticking out of his back. Then the
man *flew* out of the room! But that wasn't
the weirdest thing. When Ben stood up
to follow, he realised that he had wings
too.

———

Once he got used to flying, it didn't take
long for the two of them to get there.
Ben looked down below him and saw a

giant stadium emerge out of the clouds.
A game was already in progress.

On the pitch, the home team, the
Pearly Gate Archangels, were taking
on the visitors, the Hades Demons.
The Demons were 11 huge flaming-red
creatures with large, leathery bat-like
wings and long arrow-tipped tails. The
two teams were playing football but
it wasn't like any game Ben had seen
before. The ball looked the same but it
seemed to hover in the air. And instead
of running on a field, the players were
flying through the clouds, passing the
ball in every direction: up, down and all
around. The goal posts looked normal
enough, but they too were floating in

midair, as were the sidelines, which were marked not with white paint but glowing streaks of light.

'I can't believe you play football here,' said Ben.

'What else would we play, hopscotch?' laughed the angel. 'Go see the team manager. He's down there on the sideline.'

Ben flew down to the sideline and found the Pearly Gate manager, an old, angry-looking dude with a long white beard and a glowing ring hovering above his head.

'You the new striker?' he grunted. 'Well, don't just float there. Get on the field – we're behind by 530!'

'But . . .' Before Ben could finish his sentence, a pair of golden boots and white socks materialised on his feet and an Archangels' jersey appeared on his body.

'Cool,' said Ben. 'Did you say 500?'

'And 30,' finished the manager, as he signalled a replacement to the ref. 'So I hope you're good, kid. There's a lot riding on this game!'

As Ben flew onto the field, he glanced up at the huge scoreboard hovering above the main grandstand.

It read, 'Home: 1 000 001; Away: 1 000 531; First half: 900 years, 222 days, 5 hours, 33 minutes, 22 seconds.'

'Hey newbie!' shouted one of the

Archangels players. Ben saw a tall, muscular angel calling him over. He had jet-black hair and fierce eyes that burned like blue flame. 'I'm Mike, the Archangels' captain and midfielder,' he said. 'You ready to kick some Demon butt?'

'I guess,' said Ben.

'Just watch out for their fire bolts.'

'Fire bolts?' asked Ben. 'But you can't get, you know, killed here, can you?'

'Of course not,' said Mike. 'You're immortal now. You'll just get burnt to a crisp!'

'Oh, right,' said Ben. 'Do *we* have any special powers?'

'Well, you can try giving them a sonic blast with your angelic voice but just be careful of your aim.'

'Watch out for demon fire bolts and be careful with the sonic voice blast. Got it,' said Ben. 'When do I start?'

'Right now!' said Mike.

The Demons had just scored so it was a Pearly Gates kick-off. Mike took it and quickly passed the ball to the Archangels' lightning-quick winger, Uri. Uri burst through the Demons defence, switching the ball from one foot to the next before flicking it back to another Archangel, Gabe, who then set up a cross for Ben.

But it was hard to time a kick on the floating ball and focus on flying at the same time. Ben overflew the pass and a snarling demon snapped it up and tore away through the clouds. Ben chased

him but the demon turned and spat
a scorching fire bolt straight from his
mouth. Ben had to twist his body midair
to avoid the bolt but his wing got in the
way and a few of his feathers were singed
black.

That was close! thought Ben.

A moment later Gabe intercepted a
pass and flew away with the ball. He drew
in two Demons defenders, then passed

the ball out to Ben. This time Ben was better at controlling the ball in the air. He juggled it back and forth between his feet and lined up a shot at goal as another demon stormed towards him, his teeth dribbling smoke.

Time to try out this angelic voice thing, thought Ben.

'Laaa!' sang Ben, as loudly as he could. He felt a bit stupid singing in the middle of a football game, but the moment the note left his mouth, it felt awesome! What came out was a razor-sharp blast of sound that could push an opponent aside in an instant.

Unfortunately the demon saw it coming and ducked, which meant that the sonic blast hit Mike, who'd been backup, straight in the chest. He disappeared through a hole in the clouds.

'Oops,' said Ben. *I really need to work on my game if I'm going to compete with these guys!*

So that's exactly what he did. After a few more years of play, Ben was flying rings around the Demons and slotting goals left, right and centre. He couldn't believe how much time had passed. It felt more like minutes than years.

That was the awesome thing about playing football in heaven. You never got tired. Even if you got injured, you recovered almost straightaway. You didn't even need to stop to eat or drink.

Still, something didn't feel quite right for Ben. A few years later, the ref blew his whistle to signal halftime and the players came off the field. Ben wasn't sure he wanted to go back on. He sat miserably on the Archangels bench. He'd been playing for 100 years and he just didn't see the point of it all.

'Hey, why the glum face, newbie?' asked Mike. 'You're our leading goal scorer!'

'All we do up here is play football and try to score goals in a 2000-year-long game. What's the point? At least on Earth the goals meant something!'

'You mean you don't know what we're playing for?' asked Mike, surprised.

'No.'

'For every goal you score up here, a good deed is done on earth. Why do you think you were chosen for the team? We need the best, Ben. You see, it doesn't really matter where you are. Everything you do counts for something. Sometimes we just can't see it.'

Ben looked up at the scoreboard. It was all locked up at 1 500 000 each.

He knew what he had to do.

When the ref blew the whistle to signal the start of the second half, Ben was back out on the field.

Mike passed him the ball and Ben took on the Demons' defence, sliding between two massive red demons as they

raced towards
him, shooting
red-hot fire bolts
from their demon
mouths.

BOOF!

He landed the ball in the
far corner of the net. The choir of angels
in the grandstand went wild. Angelic
voices sang and heavenly trumpets
blared. Then the whole choir did the
Mexican wave.

And the scoreboard ticked over. The
Archangels had taken the lead.

Ben smiled. He might be facing
demons but he was in football heaven.
If he had to do something for all of

eternity, playing football would probably
be his first choice. As long as he avoided
the fire bolts, who knew how many goals
he could score between now and the end
of time?

ABOUT THE AUTHOR

Patrick Loughlin is a children's book author and high school English teacher who lives in Sydney with his wife, two daughters and hyperactive, sock-stealing spoodle. As a kid, Patrick loved sport – he just wasn't very good at it. He was quite good at writing, though, so he decided to very, very slowly become an author. Now he writes books for kids about sport. What a crazy world! Patrick is the author of the Billy Slater rugby league series and the Glenn Maxwell cricket series. One day he may write a book that's not about sport. You can visit his website at www.ploughlin.com

ABOUT THE ILLUSTRATOR

James Hart is an illustrator, comic artist and avid doodler living in the Melbourne area with his wife, kids, and dog called Shasta, who is terribly afraid of the wind and butterflies. As a kid, James was raised on a healthy diet of comics, video games, cartoons, action figures and Lego. Since beginning his journey as an illustrator in 2003 he has worked on many different projects, from toy design to book illustration. Recent projects include the animated TV series *The Day My Butt Went Psycho* and the You Choose books by George Ivanoff. When he's not drawing his favourite things (aliens, robots and monsters) he's being a dad and husband, watching movies and cartoons, drinking coffee, listening to music, reading . . . and drinking coffee. James' website is www.jameshart.com.au

OUT NOW